'Tail of a Witch' is the first book of a three part story.
Please look out for the other books:

Book 2: Tail of a Witch: The Devils Game

Book 3: Tail of a Witch: Spirit of the Five Stones

for more information go to -

www.tailofawitch.com
Instagram: tailofawitch
www.facebook.com/TailofaWitch

I

II

Information

Cover illustration and map drawing by: Paul Simpson
Story page illustrations by: Wayne Upton

ISBN: 978-1-291-88127-1

IV

13 years

The real story started 13 years ago in 2000 for a competition. The Princes Trust was supporting an event for computer games, one of the entry topics was for a 'Concept Story'. I decided I wanted to tell a scary story, as the game world was still buzzing with the first two 'Survival Horror' games that have since set a standard amongst other titles over the years. My problem, however, was how to make a zombie scary again? I solved this by making them huge like a building and the hero character small, like a cat. I figured that the point of view aspect would add a new perspective in the mix; just think how tall people really seem to a cat!

With cats and zombies ready to do battle, it seemed that Halloween would be a great setting for the story to unfold. Needing to find the perfect bad guy, I researched associated legends and found the myth behind the Jack O' Lantern, which also, at the time, became the title of the story. I now needed to create my hero, who would fight the villain, and a reason why they were a cat. I decided on a female character as I believed this would suit the cat best. Once I had this, I then looked for an appropriate name for my character and 'Fionn' stood out above any others. Although at the time I was unaware it could be pronounced differently, my first reading of the name was 'Fee-On' which felt quite feline in itself, and it stayed with me all the way even after searching many alternatives. Now I had everything, so I submitted my 500 word concept of "Jack O' Lantern."

It was a close call but I didn't win, however I had many ideas on how to expand the story and wanted to carry it on until it ran out of steam. The next phase was to create more of a background and drawings to fill out the concept to a few 1000 words, maps, character drawings and even adverts to promote it as a computer game. Printing a design for the box I submitted the ideas to various companies over the next 2 years. Those that did reply were very kind in complementing my story and designs but all of them turned me down each time.

Feeling disheartened, I began to wonder if I should give up the dream of getting my game idea recognised and move on, but I wanted to give it one last test to see if it was worth the effort as I don't believe in wasting a good idea. I sent one more box to GamesMaster magazine for their 'Designers Workshop' page and waited. In issue 134, June 2003 I had made it into the magazine. The Winners Gong that month had gone to my story. It was such a highlight to me that in reply to me asking if they thought the idea was good, they printed it as that months winner. If anything, as well as the support of my family, this gave me more reason to carry on. Later I thought I'd try again and sent the idea to PS2-Play magazine. Once again in October 2003, issue 107 I had a full page dedicated to my idea in the 'It ought to be game' section, reviewed by game developers staff.
Another win and boost to my confidence I set about spending my time at home after work drawing more and expanding the whole mini universe of Jack O' Lantern.

The project became more of a hobby now, slowly working away at it, getting anyone's thoughts and comments. I had written so much information for my game bible, I thought that, instead of writing small snippets to explain how the game plays out, I would write the entire story as a book. I fully admit I am not a writer or have ever chosen to go down the route as a profession, but this is a project that kept coming back to me time and time again. In 2005 I had written the first draft of the story. It was badly written so I didn't really let anyone read it, my method for writing it was all based on computer games and how they worked in telling a story rather than how it would read as a book. With the story complete in full and the time line of events recorded, I looked for a direction to take the idea again.

It was not long before I decided that if it couldn't be a computer game, what about a board game. Within a year I had made several incarnations of the board until I felt it was right. I then made the figures, playing cards, rule book and box design. Thanks to a small group of friends, I tweaked the rules and played the game until it was enjoyable and easy to follow within a short space of time, especially for the children's and young teenage market. Again I applied to several companies but there were no takers. At the end of this process though I did realise one thing in a 'glass half full' kind of way, I had set out to make a board game and I had it, ready to play and hold in my hands.

After a break from the project, working on other ideas as well as finally getting some of my designs/artwork finally into a computer game (a goal of mine achieved in a small way, but achieved none the less), I came back to Jack O' Lantern in 2012, in an effort to bring the idea to a close. Firstly I decided to drop the original title altering it to something that worked better for the story and 'Tail of a Witch' became the replacement. In preparing the text for release, I once again became engrossed in the world I had created. While others helped out with proofing and corrections, I began writing plot ideas, so much so that I continued on and wrote a second book. At the time of writing this is called 'Tail of a Witch – The Devils Game' and completes a mini arc of the plot from book one.

VII

My hope is that 13 years on, from October 2000 to October 2013, that these books are available to buy and if you are reading this then I made it (and thank you for buying it), followed by the third story 'Spirit of the 5 Stones' to be released in June 2014.

As I have noted, I am not a writer and don't claim to be but I have created and completed (in a different format than first intended!) something I have thoroughly enjoyed, loved, grown with over the years and hope that others will see that in my work and enjoy it for what it is. This is a project of the heart and I hope it inspires others who read this part of the book to not give up on their dreams and recognise their own success when it happens, however small.

P.Simpson

Thanks and
Acknowledgements

I would like to say thank you to those who have helped over the years.
Even though it's a short story it has been rewritten in different ways for
different uses, from a computer game concept to a board game and now
this book.

'Rocker' John Bowler – first draft proof checking and grammar.

Sian Upton – rewrites, proofing and formatting.

Wayne Upton - in book story illustrations.

Vix, Shelby, Hayley, Suzanne and Karen and others for reading and
giving feedback.

Mark Lovatt-Harris, Digiprintuk – for the Hardcopy book proofs and
playing the board game for hours until it was right.

Martin and Louise Quinn - for all their support of the project on and off
line.

GamesMaster magazine and PS2-Play magazine - for picking my idea
over the rest all those years ago.

Finally and most importantly...

Claire - for the inspiration, marrying me, making me a daddy and everything else through life. Also for all your help and support in getting the book released xxx

To all my family, those here and those lost over the last 13 years but never forgotten, for all their support in my crazy ideas with always more yet to come!

Thank you and I love you x

X

XI

Contents

Tail of a Witch

by Paul Simpson

Prologue
Limbo

In the labyrinth of limbo, in darkness black as pitch, a speck of light no bigger than a pinprick on a drawn curtain, danced to the hum of a mumbled chant.

It swung back and forth until without warning its master drew it close. Jack held his lantern high casting his twisted shadow across the engulfing dark landscape, watching, with a wry smile as the cinders within began to glow brighter. The lantern crackled and spat as from inside its hollow body rose tiny blue sparks that gently spun into an unseen breeze.

"Yessss...At last!" he cried in triumph, lifting the lantern high and willing the cinders to breath within. Slowly, hundreds, thousands of tiny sparks emerged and sailed high into the eerie darkness, a maniacal cackle willing them aloft. From within the lantern a bright blue flame illuminated Jack's face. He grinned with evil glee as he watched the flame grow and his mouth stretched wide becoming the only smile in limbo.

Introduction
Jack

An old Irish legend grew about a man named Jack. This began near the end of his life, when he was as hated as he was despised. With his long beaten wife gone, he was a solitary soul. His misery was his only companion; the beckoning call of drink remained his only constant, the craving the only thing that could match his bitterness.

One cold and stormy All Hallow's Eve Night, the Devil appeared before Jack's deathbed. He had come for his soul. Patient and resolute, The Devil stood beside the roaring fire.
Jack had other plans. Though dying, he still had some wits left about him. He asked The Dark Lord for one last favour before passing on and so he indulged him.
His request was that the Devil could manifest into a penny, so that he may taste the drink on his lips, just one last time. With a puff of purple smoke, upon the chair placed beside the bed appeared a shiny new penny. Jack snatched the coin, placed it in his leather purse and drew a cross upon it. The Devil was trapped, a prisoner of Jack's purse. Though it would not hold for long, Jack knew it would buy him more time to live and then he would release him. Intrigued, though angered by Jack's trickery, he reluctantly agreed to Jack's bargain.

Each year, on the same night, at the same time, The Devil came for Jack, and each time, for years upon years, Jack had tricked his way into renewing a deal for his life. However, on this occasion, Jack was not so lucky. His old body could take no more. The wretched old man fell asleep and never woke again.

3

Unable to enter Heaven for his wrongs doings, Jack turned to the fires of Hell for admittance. Seizing the opportunity for revenge, The Devil refused. Jack was thrown into a place where things that must not be seen are kept, the deepest and darkest Limbo. A hollowed pumpkin with an eternally burning ember was all Jack possessed to light his way for all of his exiled eternity, so that he might catch glimpses of the horrors which inhabited.

Chapter 1
The old village mansion

A cold chill to the autumn air whistled, as the large Harvest moon shone brightly through passing wispy clouds. The light poured onto the sleepy village below. Every tile, slab and cobble was washed with silvery light, illuminated by the low misty veil that wandered the empty streets below, empty all but for the sound of two pairs of feet running toward the old mansion that stood twisted and broken upon the hillside overlooking all below it.

It was October 30th and close to midnight. Several hours earlier two teenagers had been dared by their friends to venture up to the old mansion on the hill. Everyone thought the place could be haunted, some even believed it was, but all agreed it was no place to visit late at night. No one really knew the mansion's history. Some said it had been built for a rich, eccentric gentleman many years ago, although tragedy had befallen him so he never lived there, leaving the house to rot and decay. Others said that it was built overnight by a cult who used it as a meeting place for their rituals. Either way it no longer mattered, the house was old with a morbid emptiness enough to excite any imagination into believing that there was something not quite right with the place. They glanced at one another, peering through the bars of the looming gates which stood guard over all threats to the odd abode, yet it easily opened as the two leaned on it with a deafening screech of rusty metal.

"It's open!" said the boy with surprise.

"Race you to the attic!" shouted the girl, already well on her way.

The abandoned attic was cold and damp from the crisp autumn air. The moonlight shone romantically through the broken roof tiles setting everything aglow.

Their footsteps grew louder as they climbed up to the attic. When they got to the door the girl shouted "Ha! Beat you!" pleased with herself as she turned the doorknob, which was met by a loud creak as the door opened.

The boy fumbled about for his torch as they took pause to catch their breath.

"This place gives me the creeps" he said as he lit the torch, "Let's go back to the others…"

"Hey! I can see the church clock from here" she said, glimpsing out of the gaps in the roof. "Look! It's nearly Halloween! I hope you're not afraid of ghosts!" She teased.

They figured they'd look around whilst they were there. Busy hands tore through all the old junk in dusty boxes. The boy knocked a stack over in his curiosity and on to the floor toppled a dusty old book. He knelt down, picked it up and began to sift through the pages.

"Hey! Come look at this…" he spread the book out so she could look too, as he wiped off the dusty cover to reveal its title 'Local Legends', quickly cleaning off his hands on his trousers.

"It's about our village" she pointed out. They scanned some more, when he became drawn to a page for no apparent reason and to read aloud.

'The book tells of a witch and her daughter. Disobeying a coven's rules by having a child by a mortal man and, as a way of saving themselves, they turned her over to the Witchfinder General who was visiting the village. During the struggle, the girl's father was killed whilst her mother was taken and burned at the stake. The child was never found, but it is said that to protect her daughter, the mother, using powerful magic, transformed her into a cat hoping that she would escape unnoticed and eventually break the spell to avenge her parents wrongful deaths. It is said the cat still visits the standing stones on the hill, where it is believed her mother's soul is trapped until the spirits of the five are joined

6

together… or the Reaper comes and claims his prize.'

In the distance, the church clock struck midnight. The two looked nervously at each other.

From out of nowhere a blue spark appeared before them floating in mid air. They watched in awe as another made itself visible, then another and another.

The room became alive with dancing blue sparks.

They stared on at the manifesting spectacle before them, when a faint sound of laughter started to echo around the decayed attic walls.

"I hope that was you" she whispered.

"I hope it was me too!" He nervously replied.

The pretty lights swelled and appeared to open inward, as if forming a swirling tunnel. They started to edge towards the attic door, desperate to find the handle. The look of fright on their faces intensified as the laughter drew closer and louder. They were stood side on to the sparks, when they also noticed movement. The shape of a head emerged, looking directly at the children. With a glint of joy and twisted glee, Jack pulled himself free of the doorway, stretching his long bony body as high as he could reach. The teenagers made a try for the handle again, but their attempt caused Jack to notice the rattle. His tooth-filled grin, lit red by the ember he carried, was a danger sign as much as any. Screaming in horror, they flung the door open, nearly tripping over themselves in an effort to escape the old house, whilst Jack's sinister chuckle seemed to chase them from behind.

8

Chapter 2
A deal is made

Across the street, in a nearby alleyway, a group of cats had gathered and were picking on a small black female called Fionn.

"Hey, Fionn! Tell us again how you used to be human" laughed the biggest and fattest of the cats.

With her head hung low, Fionn sat in the centre of them not knowing whether to cry or walk away.

They all chuckled apart from one, a white cat named George who made his way over to her.

"Give it a rest you lot. You're only bullying her cause she's smaller than any one of you." George turned his gaze towards the fat cat, "And it's not hard, as you're bigger than everyone here put together, you big tubster!"

The rest of the gang chuckled again, apart from the fat cat who tried to disperse his embarrassment. George turned to Fionn "Come on Fionn… let's go. We don't need to hang out with these idiots," and he shoved one of them out of the way as they left.

George and Fionn walked across to the other side of the street, Fionn fell behind, trying to leave the jokes and jibes behind her that were growing quieter from the alleyway now behind them.

"Don't listen to them Fionn" George said, "The tubby one's never been the same since he lost half his tail" trying his best to cheer his friend up. "Come on, let's see that smile of yours!"

"What would I do, if I hadn't have met you George?" smiled Fionn, giving George a furry nudge, looking at him with admiration.

Amongst all the other cats, George stood out being the only white one.

He had known Fionn since he was a kitten when she had come to his rescue. It was about six years ago, when George full with curiosity and play, had wandered from his home to chase a butterfly. He had concentrated so intensely on catching his prey, that when it had flown into the sky and was gone, he realised that he had no idea where he was, or which direction he had travelled in. This wasn't made easier when two dogs appeared and trapped him in the dead end of an alley. As he backed up against the fencing, which blocked his escape, a dark shadow of a cat leapt over him, landing between himself and his two threats. "Quickly! Climb those boxes and get over the fence!" Shouted the cat. George scrambled frantically to get to the top of the fence, then fell down the large drop over the other side with a bump. He listened to the commotion arising from the side he'd left behind, with two dogs growling and the mysterious cat hissing back. The growls turned to barks, then with a boom and a flash of light, the barks turned to whimpers as he heard the sound of large paws running away. The Cat jumped over the fence and she landed next to George.

"You ok now little guy? Where are you from?" asked the black cat.

"Hi I'm George, I…I… got lost chasing a butterfly and then those dogs showed up and… and…" Fumbled George.

"It's ok now George, they're gone," she said calmly. "I'm Fionn, would you like me to help you find where you live?"

Little George nodded and grinned at his new friend and they had remained friends ever since.

Unlike George, the other cats had never come to like Fionn, they could sense she was different and didn't want her around for that one simple reason that she didn't fit in with them. George could also sense Fionn was different but he didn't care. She was his best friend and because of this friendship the other cats mostly ignored or stayed away from them both, which was fine with George as he was going to stick by her no matter what.

Over the years, George had noticed his friend becoming more and more miserable, or maybe upset, or at the very least distracted. It was hard to put his paw on, except for the fact that she had always had a spark of life within her, but recently it was fading fast.

"I know! Let's go to the old house on the hill and catch some mice! I promise I'll only hold 'em in my gums!" suggested George with his toothless grin, which made Fionn laugh.

"Oh George, you do make me smile!" beamed Fionn.

"There you go," he said "I was beginning to miss that look. I hadn't seen it in so long!"

"I don't know what I'd do without you George."

"Well, you'd be sad and lonely," he boasted. "You'd be like those old cats you see with bits of fur missing, that scratch at you with their dirty claws and crooked teeth that..."

Fionn cut him off.

"Alright! Alright! I got the idea already!" she laughed.

They made their way to the gates of the old house when they were suddenly sidetracked by the sound of screaming which was getting louder as they approached. The cats quickly jumped to one side as the old mansion gates burst open and two teenagers screamed past running for their lives, not even noticing George and Fionn, who they nearly tripped over, as they struggled to get as far away as possible.

"Hey! Watch it you big oafs! If I was bigger, I'd... I'd..." said George. George continued to rant, but Fionn was more interested in what had disturbed the two, when she noticed the haunting light coming from the holes in the attic roof.

She set off to investigate. George still talking, turned to speak to Fionn "Don't you agree Fionn? FIONN?" She had, however already gone inside.

Racing upstairs, she pushed the old door ajar with her paw and peered into the attic space. A strange blue swirl of light was shimmering in the darkness. She stepped further into the room and noticed other lights in the corner. There were two yellow blinking orbs within a ghostlike shadow which made its way over to her. As it drew closer, it was apparent they were two staring eyes.

A male voice came from the light.

"Greetings witch" spoke the soft enticing voice whose words seemed to glide around Fionn as if each one were a misty wisp. "Who's there, how do you know of me" asked Fionn.

"I know more about you than I can tell..... for now anyway" came another wisp. "I have a proposition for you, can I take it you might be interested" he breathed.

"Well that all depends now doesn't it" came Fionn's reply, "For a start you could begin by telling me what in Hell that is" asked Fionn looking over at the swirling doorway.

"Close, but not quite in Hell. Rather an extension, much like a storage locker of unwanted items if you'll excuse my weak comparison."

Fionn looked even more confused at this answer.

"OK, so you know I'm a witch and you're saying that is a doorway to Hell's storage chest."

"Correct" came the voice.

"And what is this proposition you would like to offer me" asked Fionn.

"Simple, the doorway you see here was created by one of its tenants; I want you to put him back" requested the voice.

"Sounds a bit freaky, what exactly am I putting back and why don't you do it" she replied.

The two eyes blinked and moved a little closer "His name is Jack, a tall thin skeleton of a man. You will know him by the lantern he carries which contains a burning ember. It would seem that he has been able to harness the power I placed within the ember which keeps it eternally lit to make his escape by creating this doorway. The only way to close it is for Jack to pass back through; as the power that created it came directly from me it also means I cannot interfere."

"Ok sounds a bit different to what I normally do like chase mice and sleep, so what's in it for me" questioned Fionn.

"Very well" returned the voice, "If you complete this task I ask of you I have the power to break your mother's curse upon you."

Fionn was taken aback. For nearly four centuries she had searched for a way to break the spell, now finally she had that chance. She pondered; unsure of how this entity knew these things about her, but it was the first chance she had been given and was not about to pass it up.

"Alright!" she cried "I'm in!"

"Word of warning little Witch…Jack can only pass back as the spirit he came through as. If he were to remain here for twenty-four hours, he would take physical form and the doorway would remain open forever!"

"Oh great…as if it wasn't hard enough, you should have told me before our agreement!" she kicked the dusty floor with her paw.

"Trust me little Witch, there are far worse things in there than Jack. They were put there for a reason. If the doorway is not shut they will find their way out into this world."

"Any clues as to how I might do that, you know, me being a cat and all" Fionn asked.

"To help you I can only offer some advice, seek out the necklace your mother gave you, it has a power in it you might find useful," came the cryptic reply. Fionn, shocked at how this person knew so much, asked back, "How in Hell do you know about my mother's necklace".

"Exactly, my dear. You have until midnight and the clock is ticking" came a final wisp as the intoxicating voice faded away.

In the distance, the church bell struck once. It was 1am already. From the attic doorway, George had caught up.

"Hey, there you are! Who were you talking to?" Fionn looked at her friend and then turned her gaze back to where the strange yellow eyes had been but they were no where to be seen.

"Erm… Nobody…" Said Fionn slightly confused.

"What's the matter?" Asked George. She did not reply but was deep in thought, her mind racing with possibilities.

"Err…what? Oh…sorry…I've er…got to do something," and she ran out of the attic room.

"Hey wait up! I'll come with you…wherever that is!" cried George trying to keep up. The two cats ran out of the mansion grounds, through the village streets, towards the fields and across the stone bridge that stretched over the river.

Chapter 3
Witch Stones

George caught up with Fionn who had stopped at the base of the hill.
"So, where are we going?"
"To the old shack" Fionn replied, pointing with her head.
"Why?" George quipped, he wanted answers. For well over 350 years
Fionn had lived and slept in the safe haven of the little shack, but it had
lost that comfort factor in the current predicament.
"I need my mother's necklace!" she cried. "I must find my necklace!"
George rolled his little green, crescent moon eyes, "Fionn, not the witch
thing again!"
"I knew you never believed me!" Fionn ran ahead, hurt and angry at the
discredit of her best friend.
George, regretting his quick tongue, tried to catch up with her, he huffed
and panted along the way hoping to go and make amends.

The soft breeze in the air was tapping against the wooden frame of the
shack as Fionn peered inside. The events of the night raced through her
head, as she turned her attention to the thought of her mother. For the
first time in years she began to recall noises and smells of memories past
from her youth as a young girl of seven and she tried to breath it all in.
She opened her eyes to look around the dark shack, remembering how it
stood as her home, long before her feline sentence. The aroma of her
mother's cooking on the stove and the sound of her father chopping
wood outside started to come alive, invading her senses with
overwhelming heartbreak which she clung on too just to feel them close
to her once more.
"Hey! What are you doing?" said the ever-inquisitive George. Fionn was

quickly brought back to the real world and shook the past off.

"Hey, you scared me!" Fionn cried at George, startled, heart racing and disappointed to have woken from her dream state.

"Sorryyyy… Didn't mean to make you jump" George said, drawing a big smile that made him so easy to forgive. "Hey look who I found outside while you were in here, doing whatever!"

"Who?"

"He can help us find that thing you're after, a neckl…"

"A necklace! Now who's here?"

In strolled a large shadow that drew closer to reveal a huge jaw and slobbering tongue which gave a wet, happy welcome to the two cats.

"Arnie?" Fionn called.

The large German Shepherd came into view by the streaming moonlight that made its spectacle through a broken pane.

"Hey! How you doing big guy?" Fionn beamed at the sight of him and rubbed her head against his giant rusty coloured legs, reassured and overwhelmed to see him.

"WOOF!" said Arnie with excited volume.

Fionn and George had known Arnie since he was a puppy when his owners moved in to the village a few years back. They would sneak into the yard when his humans were not about and play together to keep him company. It was an odd trio but a good one nonetheless and Arnie had become a dear friend to them both. Although to a human or other animal he seemed mean being obviously much larger and intimidating than most dogs in the village, Fionn and George knew their friend had a soft side he would only show when they were around.

"Aww thanks George" Fionn said forgiving her friend.

"Look Fionn, we're your friends and this witch thing, if you believe what you say, then it's good enough for us, right Arnie?"

Arnie nodded his head frantically, with more drops of drool hitting the dirty floor, whilst George felt happy to have put things right with Fionn having redeemed himself.

"So a necklace right? Gotta make use out of this big fella!" chuckled George.

"Yeah, a necklace. It's kinda small, polished and pebble shape with orange streaks running through it. I used to wear it as my collar, but one day I took it off, having lost hope of finding what I needed and it dropped through a gap in these floorboards," said Fionn, directing with her paws.

"Right ok, if Arnie finds something with your scent on it Fionn, we can start digging. Let's do this!"

Arnie began his search, sneezing and coughing from the accumulated dust, which clung to the memories of the place. Fionn and George watched him intensely as he covered the floor from wall to wall. Suddenly, Arnie stopped and barked, going berserk. The two cats ran over, making their way past the dog's manically wagging tail. Fionn peered through the crack in the floor.

"See anything?" asked George.

"Something shiny I think, I can just about see it," as she popped her slender leg through the hole, trying to reach with her paws and claws. "Yes! Got it!" She cried with glee.

"So why did you let it go in the first place?" wondered George.

"I gave up, it was a constant painful reminder, so I chose to lose it, but now... I need it and, until the spell is broken, it can help me focus my powers."

"So that's why you've been down?" Rather than a reply, feeling too guilty to muster words, she threw George and apologetic smile. She gracefully slipped the necklace around her neck, thanked her two furry friends and then made her way into the cool night air.

"I've got to go and see somebody, I'll be back in a while..." And she made her way off with a renewed spring to her pounce.

17

George could look on feeling a little more light hearted as he hadn't seen her this alive in a long time. He would wait for her and help her in any way he could just too be close to her happy mood.

Arnie nudged him as if he was thinking the same thing.

"I know big fella, I worry about her too…"

"Woof!"

"Wanna play some ball?"

"Woof!" came the response in agreement and the two ran down the hill.

Fionn had made her way over the next hill where five large upright stones stood. Amongst the litter of magazines and empty drink cans that visitors had left, were the five black obelisks that stood out of the ground in a circular arrangement. Their etched markings though still evident, had faded over the centuries from the battering of wind and rain. At the centre of the stone circle the ground was bare with no grass cover. Village lore had named these monoliths the 'Witching Stones', as it was believed that no living thing could grow inside the circle. Fionn bowed her head with recognition, respect and love and waited as she used to do for the presence of the necklace to summon the power in the stones. She walked inside the confines of the circle and her necklace began to glow blue, synchronizing to the pulsing light that was emerging from the middle of the stones, with every second it's brightness increased to reveal a human form.

"Hello my loving daughter," spoke the figure within the light.

"Hello mother, it's been a while." Voice shaking whilst tears were welling.

"I have waited so long for this moment to arrive my little girl. You must know that events are now in motion that cannot be undone. It is your destiny and our very existence that you are fighting for tonight, for if you fail this task then we will both cease to exist."

"Mother, I'm sorry I've not been here for a long while, I gave up, but

18

things have changed, I know you can sense something is happening. Please tell me what I must do?" Fionn asked with an emotive mix of sorrow, fury and desperation. The voice from the attic never said anything about failure directly affecting her and she hissed at the thought of being duped, but she had to shrug off the anger so she could focus and listen.

"Its ok Fionn, I understand. You always were a sweet child and your abilities far surpassed mine. You were never any problem and always there to lend a hand, ever curious to learn and grow and that is why you will succeed tonight.

The person you seek is named Jack. He will cause a series of events tonight that will ultimately affect you and me. These Witching Stones contain the wisdom of the past and the knowledge of the future. As long as I am trapped within them they will help me to foresee the paths that are set before you this very eve. Know that this is where your true journey begins." Her mother continued.

"If you know what needs to be done, please, tell me mother." Fionn returned.

"I cannot reveal what will happen tonight. It is forbidden sweet one, however, I can guide you but first I must give you a gift."

Fionn looked on intensely.

"Quick child! Bring the necklace into the light."

Fionn walked forward until it was possible for her mother's spirit to brush the necklace around her neck. It turned a deep hue of orange as it absorbed her mother's power.

"Now become the young woman you should have been!"

Fionn withdrew from the stones as the necklace continued to glow fervently.

"Use your gifts, tap into the power of the pendant. Choose the form you wish to be and become it! Now concentrate child… Imagine walking as a human…"

The orange glow throbbed and pulsated with more life and energy. Small sparks of light fizzed and crackled like a firework, focusing their magic dance around Fionn's form. Their motion started quick and chased each other until she could no longer be seen. The colours now ran vertically, sparkling into the air, as if on ascent, to reveal a young seven year old child in a raggedy dress.

Hands stretched out, toes wriggling on the floor, Fionn was once more her old self again. The feeling was indescribable. She had waited for this for so long and now it was suddenly here, she just had to cling onto it. Funnily enough, she missed her black velvet coat to keep her warm as the cold started to hit her snow-white skin allowing it to seep in to the bone.

A magazine, blown from a bin, was amongst other litter left by teenagers who visited the stones to see if they could witness a ghost. It lay on the floor near to her new feet as it's pages blew in the wind. A photograph of a gothic beauty in punkesque stripy tights caught her eye along with a black outfit on the following pages looked pretty appealing to her.

"That's exactly what I want," she said to herself, "and I think I need to look a little bit older now given my true age."

With a fizz of sparks that twirled around, Fionn began to grow and her ragged clothing transformed.

She admired her now older teenage modern self, looking stunning in her black tank top, short black dress and purple and green stockings that accentuated her human legs down to her buckled boots. Feeling good about herself, she remembered to draw her attention back to her mother.

"How will I get Jack back to the portal?" she asked with a newly determined spirit, growing stronger with every second of resolve. "I know very little magic mother. If I don't complete the task I'll cease to exist, no life, no death, just gone."

"I acquired my powers by accident daughter, yet I bore you, so these

20

powers you have inherited naturally are stronger than my own, even when you were still a child. Your power source is similar to the token ember Jack carries, yet it has evolved within you. That is why it is you who was picked tonight. Only you are strong enough to stop him. Use the spellbook I created as your guide until the time comes when you no longer need it. I'm sorry I can't help you in the same way I had assistance discovering my powers."

Fionn paused to soak it all in.

"When you are strong enough you must force Jack into the open. Travel to the Village Hall. At the rear of the building that leads to the forest's edge, lies a pumpkin patch. Collect six pumpkin seeds and combine them with the growing spell in the book. Then, before midday, you must plant them, any later they will not have time to grow to full size… Only magically grown pumpkins can be used with the 'Expel' incantation, which is the only thing that can flush Jack out of hiding if you are to succeed in your mission."

"How do I do that?"

"Go to our home Fionn and search within the fireplace for the book. Look for the longest brick and remove it, it is behind there." Her mother revealed.

Her light began to fade and so did her voice, so she spoke quickly, "Unless your spell is broken, you cannot hold human form without the power in the necklace. I love you my daughter. Return to me when the task is complete, for there is a second task that I must ask of you."

"I love you mother, I'll do us both proud, father too…" A lonely tear that shone like crystals from the moon's light streaked down her porcelain cheek.

Chapter 4
First meeting

As much as Fionn liked her human form, she could travel much quicker as a cat, so she transformed and ran for the Village Hall, which also served as the local library. Following her mother's instructions, she went around the back of the building to the pumpkin patch and found herself staring at them, willing them to open. Her necklace burst with colour again as her powers began to grow. With a crunch, pop and splat, the pumpkins exploded, exposing the seeds she needed to collect. The necklace magically drew them in, storing them safely for later.

A light was coming from one of the Village Hall windows.

"Who could be in there at this time of night?" She immediately went to check. The rear security door had been forced open and was now creaking in the breeze as it swung. She stepped inside, making her way down the hallway to where the light seemed to be coming from. She entered the main hall and there, by the fireplace, stood a tall, ghostly white, spindly figure of a man that turned to face her.

"Hello little cat and your name is…?" he asked in jest not expecting an answer.

"Fionn" she spat.

"A talking cat?" He laughed. "And what magic is this?" He had to bend over with the hilarity.

"Have things changed so much since I was last here" he quizzed with himself? "Oh, wait, I'm sorry, it's just when you've seen what I've seen, nothing surprises you any more…" His chuckling started to fade and he caught more breath as his demeanour changed for the worse "So little one… Where are you from" came the words hissing from his mouth as he approached Fionn, suspicious of anything and anyone.

24

"I live here, always have. I used to be human until my mother turned me into a cat to escape The Witchfinder when he came to the village. So, how about you?" Fionn took a few steps back away from him.

Jack's emotions changed again to become more inquisitive. "That's a pretty intriguing story but mine is an even stranger tale, or should I say tail?" He laughed again as Fionn looked on, unable to read his erratic changes of mood as he continued to speak.

"Well my dear, I died a long time ago. I played a few tricks, dabbled in magic here and there, then when I died my soul was cast into the darkest limbo, the one where all the horrid things you should never see are kept. This lantern was my punishment, so I could catch glimpses of those grotesques, but… I got wise and escaped. I was ready for him, made plans for my escape long before he trapped me. The last laugh will be mine" and he gave a laugh at the thought that his own genius plan had worked.

"You're Jack!" She cried without thinking. Jack's face turned to horror as she called his name.

"He sent you, didn't he? DIDN'T HE?" He lunged at Fionn, swiping her with his arm and knocking her clear across the hallway. The bump caused her to change back to human form as a reflex so she could fight back, but it was too late, he'd already escaped. The door clicked shut with an echo that filled the empty hall.

"Damn it" she said under her breath.

Chapter 5
Human!

It was a long, slow walk back to the shack as she made her way tripping and stumbling, unaware that she was upright on her own two feet after the blow from Jack.

She pushed the door hard and it opened with a bang. Entering the room Fionn positioned herself in front of the fire place. With a small rotation of her finger, the fire lit up and the shack was warmed by dancing flames. Fionn lay down and gave a feline stretch on top of the old rug and yawned. The thoughts of what had happened back at the hall raced though her head.

Many minutes later, she heard somebody approach from the path outside, when George entered the shack. He was completely unprepared for the surprise. A human lay on the floor before him. He crept further around the room for a better look. Moving slowly his paw came to rest on a loose floorboard which emitted a loud creek. He quickly cowered behind a small table, hoping to go unnoticed so he could look for an escape.

Fionn caught a glimpse of his fuzzy white tail.

"George, hey George! Is that you?"

George became even more scared, how on earth did this human know his name and furthermore how come he could understand them? Deciding that he would rather not find out, he made a bolt for the door.

"George, Wait!" Fionn cried realising she had forgotten her human self. She closed the door just in time, she had always been faster than George, but he was quicker at looking at places to escape, he locked his eyes on the window.

"George, George, just wait a second!" She waved her hand which closed all the window shutters. George was in a panic now. Having nowhere to hide, he forced himself into a corner, arching his back. His claws extended and his mouth hissed. He could put up a fight when he put his mind to it, yet Fionn calmly knelt down.

"George, it's me, Fionn!" His head dropped to one side, but his claws were still at the ready. "Come on! How many humans do you know that speak cat? Here let me show you something…" He lowered his back but his claws remained poised.

"I'll explain everything to you if you promise not to run away." Laying her hand over her necklace, a slow shimmer of light surrounded her body and the blinking flickering lights encircled her once more. She shrank into the swirling colour until all traces of the large human figure had disappeared. Stood before him, on four legs instead of two, was a small black cat George immediately recognised as Fionn.

"See I told you there was nothing to be afraid of."

"All this time…every second of it…you were telling the truth!" Babbled George, trembling beneath his furry coat.

"Yes. I never lied to you George. It's always been the truth and now I have the chance to put things back to how they should be."

"Does this mean you're going to be leaving?" He asked disappointedly.

"Yes, I'm afraid it might. There is something I have to put right and tonight I have a chance to break the spell and do that."

"Wow, I know you said you were over 300 years old but I just took that as cats years" said George with a grin. "Okay I'll help you. Just promise me one thing? Promise that you won't forget about your friend, the loveable rogue who's always there for you?" He asked with a cheeky grin across his white face.

"You don't have to worry. I'll never forget my best friend."

"Good, then I'm with you all the way," pledged George. "So explain to me what's going on and is it anything to do with what's happening in the village?"

"In the village?" Asked Fionn puzzled.

George jumped onto the window ledge, staring out to the village below. Fionn joined him. In the distance, at the bottom of the hill the village seemed to have come alive. People were screaming and shouting whilst running away from their homes in fear. It soon become apparent to Fionn that the doorway which Jack had opened, was affecting more than just the old mansion house.

"I'm not prepared damn it! I need more time!"

"No problem, what do you need?" Asked George.

Fionn morphed with the use of the necklace. She concentrated hard and soon the strange light returned and traced over her feline body, when emerging from the twirling light, she was human again.

Fionn crouched by the dusty fireplace. She looked for the longest stone in the wall just as her mother had told her to. She found it and scraped away the years of dust and soot, finding the edges she pulled the stone out. Just as her mother had said, there behind the hole in the wall, was the hidden spell book. She picked it up. It had been compiled by her mother, many, many moons ago when Fionn was just a little girl. It was full of rhymes, illustrations, spells, chants and descriptions of encounters with creatures which her mother had been dedicated to recording. All of her knowledge and secrets were bound within these pages.

George sat and watched in amazement waiting for what would come next.

"Right, let's get started."

The hours passed as George and Fionn worked through the night making preparations for the task ahead. He helped Fionn by collecting all the items he could find and carry in his mouth, as required in the lists of the book's pages.

Fionn moved the furniture, put the ingredients together and was ready to start mixing in an old rusty cooking pot. As the items were thrown in, the potion was forming and the magic was growing. Sparks of vivid colour burst into the air like a firework display and the colourful smoke plumed through the windows, doorway and chimney. From down in the village the old shack looked like a spectacle to behold, alight and sensational, If anyone had time to notice that was. In the gardens and in-between the houses, people were still running scared, being hunted and chased by spooks, ghouls and other creatures, who had been spat out of Limbo and emerged through the portal door and were out to cause chaos.

After several hours Fionn and George were finished.
"What do we do now?" Asked George.
"Now? Now I drink this and we see if it works before the sun comes up and those 'things' down there go into hiding."
"I was afraid you'd say that." George turned to the door with Fionn following him. When he turned to look at her, he saw the worried, twisted expression on her face. "There's no way you're leaving me behind." He said. "It wouldn't be safe to go down there alone. Besides, you could do with another pair of eyes, and... and I can help you" he pleaded.
There was no room or time for debate.
"Okay, you win! Just be careful and let me handle things, ok?" She said with a smile and the two friends set off down the hillside.

Chapter 6
Test of power

The village was in chaotic uproar. The flashing lights from their once quaint homes drove them into the streets screaming causing people to lose both their minds and wits in the unfolding events around them. Doors and windows banging open and ghouls screeching, all adding to the nightmare. Ghostly red, blue and green soul orbs chased them in their attempted frenzied escape and there was no sign of things slowing down anytime soon.

Fionn and George walked through the village gingerly, hoping to remain hidden and avoid the unfolding drama. Fionn found a large Oak tree to stand by while she prepared herself. She closed her eyes and began to concentrate whilst the necklace began to do its thing. Lifting her hands slowly, a spark of light crackled around her bewitching fingers which began to grow brighter as the power intensified. With a final surge, Fionn's eyes opened wide, white over and full of wild energy at the sight of the circular power source she had called forth within her hands. George's jaw dropped, "Ermm, I'll wait here then?" He had never seen anything like it before. Fionn however, had not heard him as she kept her train of thought on the task before her.

She stepped out from her hiding place and leapt into action. A jolt of power flew from her fingers like a lightening bolt, then another, then another like beautiful but deadly electric streams. The orbs were happily terrifying the village residents until they sensed Fionn's magic and changed direction to launch their attack on the little witch like a swarm of angry wasps. Fionn stayed determined and kept launching her attacks to defeat the orbs.

The street fell silent at last as the villagers scrambled to their feet and ran for their homes not knowing who or what to be more afraid of.

"Not bad for a beginner Fi, I could have helped but everyone's gotta start out somewhere right?" said George.

The luminescent light faded from Fionn, she appreciated and smiled at what George had just said. The two set off again when George stopped suddenly.

"Hey! Hey! Did you hear that?"

In the distance, the sound of horribly distorted children's laughter started to get louder. George and Fionn readied themselves for what was obviously coming their way. The sound of fighting and madness came closer. As he looked around, George thought he had spotted movement.

"There!" he pointed to the left. Fionn turned to look finding a small gang wearing 'Trick or Treat' masks approaching. They appeared to be childlike moving in a mischievous yet menacing manner. They drew closer and spread out until they had the pair fully surrounded. Fionn studied them. These weren't children at all; they were some sort of strange creature she had never seen before.

In fact, there were two kinds of creature. The first, seemed to be male, with a large rounded mask of a skull tied to their heads with leather straps to secure it in place. The second type loosely resembled a girl. It wore a devil mask and carried a burning pitchfork, which it seemed to control like a sort of small flame thrower.

"So, who's the trick and who's the treat?" laughed Fionn sarcastically. Without hesitation, one of the skull masks stepped forward to look at Fionn for what felt like a lifetime but what was in fact seconds. The creature inhaled over-dramatically, forcing his mask to open up, almost splitting in half at the mouth. A strong blast of air bellowed forth, knocking George and Fionn off their feet and across the ground as they stumbled and rolled onto a grass verge.

"I guess you're the Tricker?" She spoke slightly winded from the attack.

32

"George, wait here and keep an eye out, I'm just going to teach these 'Things' a lesson in manners" said Fionn.

"They're all yours, I'll just wait here then till your done?" Came his reply. She climbed to her feet and went back to the centre of freaks that found their fall quite amusing and seemed to cackle amongst themselves at their own mischief. The Trickers prepared for another blast whilst the Treaters aimed their pitchforks.

"Wanna play rough do you?" Asked Fionn, poking fun at the creatures. "Well, Bring it!"

Her hands and eye's became white with her powers as she discharged a bolt with such ferocity that it knocked the first creature clear over a nearby fence. George, though petrified, stood and looked at his friend with newfound respect whilst the fighting raged on. Keeping a watchful eye out he saw two of the creatures whispering and then retreating to a nearby alleyway.

"No you don't!" He roared.

Fionn stood triumphant over the fallen creatures, proud of her work and pleased with her awesome powers.

"George, GEORGE, where'd you go?"

"Fionn! Over here, quick!"

She raced over to where George was waiting "Did you see that? I WON!" She beamed with pride to her friend.

"Well, while you were playing, two escaped. Luckily I clocked their escape and followed them over to the mansion grounds. I think you'd better come with me." George turned and ran with Fionn close behind.

34

Chapter 7
Trick and Treat

They ran past the houses and into the clearing until the Trick and Treater came into view by the side of the field. Orbs swarmed round the foul creatures in a crazed-tornado.

The Tricker opened his mask with a deep inhale as spirals of orb souls were sucked into his mouth. This made the Tricker stronger and it grew until it was the size of a house. The Treater squealed with laughter as the super Tricker bent down and with a swipe of his enormous hand lifted the Treater high above the ground. The Tricker, now holding The Treater with its burning pitchfork up to its mouth, opened its mask once more and blew across the Treaters flame sending a huge dragon-like breath of fire in Fionn's direction.

George and Fionn looked at one another in disbelief.

"Any ideas?" asked Fionn.

George pondered for a moment, "Nope, I'm all out on this one."

At the same moment the gigantic Tricker, now standing over 40 feet high, began to charge towards them.

"I know," said George, "I'll distract him so you can get in a clear shot."

George ran as fast as his little furry legs could carry him aiming right in between the legs of the giant. Fionn tried to stop George's foolish plan but it was already too late, she couldn't grab him in time. He was halfway across the field as the Tricker closed in on him. Fionn drew on all the magic within herself that she could muster. She stepped into the open ground directing a huge blast at the Tricker's back.

The bolt nearly knocked the Tricker off its feet as it staggered about, struggling to quickly regain it's balance. Turning its gaze away from

George and now onto Fionn the giant charged straight for her. Jumping out of the way of the charging creature Fionn landed with a roll turning to see as the huge beast hit the tree she was standing next too. Unable to stop in time the Tricker stumbled and fell face first into the soft grassy ground, all the while the Treater screamed as the clutch around it tightened in the fall. Fionn launched more shots hitting the Tricker square on the side of its head, causing the mask to crack as several of the trapped spirits escaped.

"That's it" shouted George from the other side of the field. "It's the mask! If it's broken, it can't hold the orbs and it will lose power! You have to break the mask Fionn!"

She looked for herself and, sure enough, the Tricker was holding its hand over a damaged side of its mask so the orbs could not escape. The giant held up the Treater to defend itself. Once again the Tricker blew a breath, sending out a blast that burned the grass scorching its way towards Fionn. With no time to escape she crossed her wrists and held them out away from herself as the fire hit her.

"Nooooooooooooooooo!!!" screamed George helplessly, hardly daring to look as the flames engulfed her body.

The fiery blast cleared and the Tricker and George looked at Fionn. She stood in a spherical shield of energy that had protected her from the heat of the blast.

"That all you got? Well, have some of this!"

Her eyes turned white and she unleashed a volley of shots at the Tricker's head sending the monster reeling from the attack. Each hit smashing away at its mask until it finally shattered in a burst of light. The orbs escaped into the air with a scream of a thousand dammed souls regaining their freedom. The giant dropped to its knees and stared at Fionn, then, with a deafening sound its body exploded with a vivid flash of red, yellow and purple sparks, leaving the Treater, which it had held in it's hand, to fall to the floor with a thud. Weak and shaking under its own

36

weight, the Treater struggled to hold itself up. Exhausted, still on its hands and knees it turned its head slowly only to see a pair of black buckled boots standing next to it. Looking down into its dead eyes, Fionn swung back one foot and with all of her strength kicked the Treater hard in the mask, which, similarly to its companion's, cracked and splintered, ultimately exploding in a burst of colour and light.

Fionn felt the rays of warmth from the rising sun upon her face, as the dawn's golden light forced its way through the dark storm clouds above. "I need you to do me a favour," said Fionn to George, trying to catch her breath as George looked up at her.
"These seeds need to be planted near the river bank by the Water Mill." She held out a small silk bag, which George took in his mouth.
"The damp ground and the potion in the bag should help them to grow, just pour it over the ground around them. It'll be safe to go there while the sun is out. I'm gonna go back to the shack and take a little rest," she said to George "I've got a feeling it's going to be a very long night."

Chapter 8
Dreams of the past

Back at the shack Fionn had changed back to her cat form and settled into her usual sleeping place. Although she could have stayed human, she thought it could be difficult to fully integrate after three centuries of being a cat. Tonight she couldn't take any chances either but now she desperately needed sleep to regain her spent energy levels. She curled up, her whiskers and paws twitching as she fell into a deep, deep sleep. In her slumber, memories came flooding back, patchy at first but as her sleep deepened they became more vivid. As usual, she remembered 'that day'. She relived the moments of the fateful day that changed her whole life. She was back to the 17th century, everything in slow motion, each frame being a picture and echoing with noise.

Fionn was seven years old again, playing on a tree swing her father had made for her, watching the sunset over the horizon. As she gazed from her vantage point, a warm light caught her eyes coming from the windows of their home.

"Fionn, it's time to come in. It's time to eat sweetheart."

Fionn ran to the doorway and flung her arms around her mother's neck but the dream never allowed her to see her mother fully, only glimpses and blurs, hands reaching out to hold her, a lock of red hair blowing in the breeze, a voice that whispered "I love you" as they embraced.

"How about wearing this for luck tonight while I finish my work?" Her mother took off her necklace and fastened it around Fionn's neck.

"Come on now, go wash up before we eat and no playing with your dolls again."

Her mother returned to the stove to finish cooking whilst Fionn cleaned up from her adventures outside. She ran into the room to do as her mother had asked but caught sight of her dolls on the chair. Hoping her mother would not notice, she quickly waved her hands about the air causing them to softly glow with magic, as the girl and boy dolls rose to their feet and began to dance with each other. Fionn quietly giggled with delight as they swayed to the sound of the rhythmic beat of the axe her father was using to cut wood outside. He was a tall, well built man with long hair which he often tied back while he worked. She loved how he would often play with her after his work had finished for the day. In the evening he would show off for his little girl by juggling and spinning his axe as he chopped the wood to make the evening fire. This night was different somehow, she knew something was happening when she heard other voices outside and her father's getting louder. It was the sound of an argument that quickly escalated into a scuffle. Fionn peeked through the slight gap in the room's open door and saw the front door of the cabin burst open. Several strange men, not from the village, with burning torches entered. Her father attempted to stop and reason with them but he was outnumbered and deliberately ignored. Grabbing his axe he began to fight off the intruders. During the ensuing fight to block their advance, one of the group sneaked up behind him with a blade in his hand and stabbed him. Her father fell to the floor, still reaching out trying to stop them but his strength was fading along with his life. All he could do was look on helplessly, unable to protect the two people in his life he valued above anything and who were about to be taken from him. Two of the men grabbed Fionn's mother by her hair and dragged her away screaming. Amongst the chaos, but still thankfully hidden, a tear fell down Fionn's cheek as she watched her father slip away. She could hear her mother chanting strange words and realised it was some form of spell being cast, as she was no stranger to magic.

Her mother had gained her powers by some unknown accident years before, although she never spoke of it. From this Fionn was born naturally possessing her magical gift. This developed as she grew, much to her father's distress, as he did his best to hide both his daughter's and wife's gifts. Although he accepted their abilities, he was merely a mortal man. He made up for his lack of powers, however, with love and affection for his family.

Fionn began to feel a strange sensation as her mother's spell was meant for her. She fell to her knees, clutching her stomach, as the room started to spin. When it stopped, the world seemed much larger than before. She continued to look through the gap, when she saw The Witchfinder General enter the kitchen. He noticed the back room door ajar and stepped forward to fully force it open. The door swung wildly hitting Fionn and knocking her over, she sprawled to regain her balance. The Witchfinder bent down and picked her up. Fionn hissed loudly and with a lunge, scratched his face. He flinched trying to protect himself as she wriggled herself free from his grasp. Quickly adapting to her new feline form, she landed on her four new feet. She ran as fast as she possibly could through the front door jumping over the lifeless body of her father, who lay in a crimson pool of blood. She had no time to grieve and she wasn't safe here so she carried on running, heading for the forest. After a good distance, she took one last solitary glance behind her to find her mother, although she immediately wished she hadn't. Her mother was set alight on a wooden stake, her flesh charred and deafening screams of pain rising into the red smoke filled sky.

Suddenly and from nowhere, the now-rotting face of the Witchfinder jumped into view.

"I'm coming for you!" He screeched, pointing at Fionn.

Fionn awoke from the painful memory short of breath and tearful; she shook her head trying to get rid of the sight of The Witchfinder General and the sound of her mother's cries.

She jumped to the window and watched as the sun began to set over the

41

horizon. The church clock was illuminated and read 4.30. She knew that as soon as the last drop of light had disappeared, the trouble would begin.

"Let's finish this" she thought as she counted down the time.

Unseen by Fionn, a dark shadow loomed around the rear of the old shack. The bright red sun burned Jack's shadow against the wooden frame. Jack lifted his lantern closely to his face and gazed deeply into it. The lantern's magic embers revealed Fionn's dream to Jack.

"So my dear…" he hissed "There is something that you fear after all and I know just where to find it."

44

Chapter 9
The grave meeting

Fionn was plagued by her nightmare and felt she had to put the matter to rest whilst she had use of her human form. She wanted to know where The Witchfinder General was buried, so she set her course for the library to check the local history records. By the time she had reached the bottom of the hill, the last ray of light dissolved into the night sky. After the earlier events, any villagers had either left or barricaded themselves securely in their homes. This also meant that the local hall, which accommodated the library and from which Jack had appeared and escaped earlier, could also be locked. Wandering around the building she was pleased to discover that the back door was still open.

Making her way inside, she saw that it was just as chaotic in there. Tables and chairs had been carelessly thrown around, books had been torn apart and the whole place stood in miserable disarray. Within the hall the fireplace still gave off warmth from the fire that Jack had started. Fionn changed back to her human self to make it easier to sift through the debris to find the information she was seeking. Bathed in the firelight Fionn noticed that the rain began to fall outside drumming against the windows.

The gruelling task of checking book after book after an hour meant that Fionn had only tidied one room. She searched on when, suddenly, a flash of light passed the window. It was a sphere of light to be more exact. What she first thought to be lightening looked now more like the ghostly orbs she had seen earlier disturbing the village. This one, however, was of a golden colour, at least she thought so before her attention was then brought to another, closer cause for concern. A clatter from the balcony above distracted her, it sounded as if something had fallen or was pushed. Fionn looked around but could see nothing. Deciding to resume her reading, as luck would have it, she found exactly what she was looking for. In the dusty hand-scribed pages someone had eulogised the one she sought. She read eagerly about his life and the places he had supposedly cleansed, surprised to discover that this self appointed Witchfinder General, had lived out his last few remaining years in her village and was laid to rest in the local churchyard.

"So you're here, after all this time I finally know."

Another clatter rung out from above.

"Hello?" She yelled.

A shadow inked itself against the walls and a nearby window, "Hey who is this?" She asked with an air of caution.

As the sound of footsteps raced across the wooden flooring, Fionn stood up slowly from the table where she sat. She began to creep towards the noise when another drum of footsteps came from behind her. Turning quickly, there was nothing there, then another quick flash of shadow followed. Fionn felt as if a dozen eyes were watching her and, in truth, they probably were. Another race of footsteps came towards her and then stopped abruptly. She jumped back with alarm. Standing no taller than her waist was a nasty looking imp. It's hoofed feet tapped on the floor, as it stood watching Fionn with its goat like yellow eyes sticking out from its elongated and protruding head. She waited to see if it would move again.

A second imp jumped down from the balcony and landed next to her. Fionn turned with magic at the ready, when the first imp snatched the necklace from around her neck with its long pointy fingers. In the blink of an eye, Fionn was back to being a cat. Without her necklace, her magic and hope was lost. Now it was Fionn who was waist high to the imps. They hissed and giggled at her through small and broken razor-sharp teeth. Just before their exit, the first one held up the necklace triumphantly then disappeared into the black stormy night. Fionn, now seemingly powerless, had only one thing she could do; chase them.

The imps had headed east towards the bridge over the river, aiming for the cemetery. Fionn followed in pursuit, trying to keep up as best she could. As they reached the church grounds, she watched them run between gravestones and then disappear behind a large marble crypt. High up above them all, the church clock struck 6 o'clock. On the sixth chime, Fionn took a deep nervous breath before she entered the sacred ground where she now knew The Witchfinder lay. She examined each stone for his location, the Imps and her necklace would have to wait, just for now. A strange scratching noise sounded from the other side of the graveyard, like fingernails dragging on a chalkboard making Fionn shudder.

"Another damn distraction" she screeched as she went to find out what this noise was. Moving to investigate she realised that The Witchfinder's grave was now in front of her and low and behold, Jack was standing behind it. She then noticed that the Imps she had been chasing lay dead at his feet. He had been scraping his fingers against the headstone as if to lure her in. In his other bony hand he clasped her necklace which he had taken from the creatures when he killed them.

Aglow from his lantern, Jack took a side step around the grave towards her.

"I knew you'd come and you didn't let me down. There's something I want to give you."

"There's only one thing I want from you JACK!" she spat, "My necklace!"

"Tut Tut! and here I was, working so hard on my gift for you." he turned his gaze to the necklace, "I merely borrowed your pretty little kitty collar to get you here."

"Gift?" said Fionn not quite following Jack's maniacal plan.

The ground by Jack's feet started to tremble and shift.

"If I'm not mistaken…" he said with excitement, "Your gift should be here right... about....now!"

Fionn looked hard at the ground.

"I thought it'd be nice for you to see an old family acquaintance Fionn" he chuckled loud and hard.

The headstone of The Witchfinder cracked and broke apart. The earth where he was buried vibrated and the loosened wet soil pushed upwards followed by an outreached skeletal hand.

"NO! What have you done?" Shouted Fionn.

A second hand burst out from the grave pulling it's body upward finally revealing the Witchfinder's head.

"What's wrong? I thought you'd be happy to see him again, it's what you wanted isn't it?" said Jack, clearly enjoying Fionn's dismay.

A burst of energy filled the Witchfinder's body then flew from the grave and seemed to scream as the General awakened. The power rumbled across the floor, churning the dirt and toppling every headstone like dominoes. It travelled like a wave toward Fionn, catching her off guard until she was swept off her feet, violently hitting her head against a gravestone knocking her out cold.

Nearby, George and Arnie had been searching for Fionn. They had heard the commotion coming from the cemetery and decided to investigate. When they arrived they were shocked to see the rotten body of The Witchfinder closing in on Fionn.

"Hey Arnie, wanna catch a bone?" Arnie ran over to Fionn and, guarding her body with his massive size, he started to bravely bark at the decaying corpse coming towards them.

"Fionn! Hey Fionn!" yelled George "Come on, we gotta get outta here!"

Fionn woke, shook off the pain in her head and clambered onto Arnie's back, grabbing on to his collar and fur. He ran fast and hard to get them out of the hellish situation.

'WOOF!' he bellowed to George signalling that it was time to leave.
'I don't know what's going on, but this village has gone nuts!' remarked
George. 'Let's get her back to safety and quick!'
Not even looking back, the two friends with Fionn barely hanging on ran
out of the church grounds and off up the hillside towards the forest
seeking cover.
The General watched as the animals disappeared into the thick mist that
smothered the forest edge. His bones clicked and tendons stretched and
squeezed as he turned his gaze to Jack.
"And how will I find her now?" The General gargled with what little
remained of his throat.
"With this!" answered Jack, throwing the necklace to the General, who
caught it in his skeletal grip, a toothless grin on what was left of his face.
"Keep it close and she'll come looking for you."

Chapter 10
Friends together

Fionn opened her eyes and everything started to come back into focus. Her two friends were standing by her.

"Where, where are we?" asked Fionn.

"Well…err…remember a few summers ago that scout group made a tree house around the base of one of the big oaks…well ta-dah! Who thought it would have come in use, eh? Eh?" nudged George trying to make light of a very dark situation.

"Don't worry about Jack, he won't find this place, the fog was just too thick, and it was easy to lose the lumbering fool" said George trying to reassure his friend. Fionn, however, still looked understandably concerned.

"What happened to my home? Why aren't we there?"

George paused, thinking of how to phrase his next words. Outside a cold bitter wind whistled through any gaps in the hut.

"Well… we went there to find you around sunset but you had already left. Someone else was there too…"

"Jack? Was it Jack?"

"Yeah, he was there alright" said George and he paused again to look away from Fionn.

"What? What did he do George?"

"He tore the place down to the ground with that pumpkin thing he holds. Fionn, I am so, so sorry…" he bowed his head.

Thoughts ran through her brain, there was little time left and she needed to concentrate.

"The Book of Spells! Where is my mother's book?"

"Don't worry we got that covered, brought that here with us, it's over

51

there in that box." George pointed to the corner of the room with his little head.

Fionn's head throbbed again reminding her she had been unconscious. "How long was I out?" she asked.

"After you got back here its been about an hour," replied George "So who was the zombie?"

"He's coming for me and I reckon he'll have my necklace now" came the reply as she climbed to her feet.

"He? Who? What's going on? What happened back there? Come on Fionn, we deserve answers!"

Fionn's tone became irritate and defensive.

"The Witchfinder General is here. The man who killed my parents. Jack has brought him back to get me!"

"Listen Fionn, we are you friends, let us help you. We can stop him together…"

"No!" Fionn shot George down. "Not without my necklace, it's too dangerous."

"Dangerous for who? You? Me? Arnie? Tell me, please, cause I'm dying to know" said George matching Fionn's frustration. "And, might I add, you're the one who just got rescued!"

"This is my one shot"

"One shot? At what? Losing your friends? Stop being so human headed! We're all involved now, not just you! What, nothing to say?" George turned to walk away. "Fine! Have it your way, be all by yourself. But you know what? There'll be a time you need your friends and they won't be there!"

Arnie looked over at Fionn and gave a whimper of concern.

"Come on Arnie, we know when we not wanted."

"Woof!" said Arnie sadly and went to join George.

Fionn watched her friends walk into the foggy night, George's voice fading as they got further away.

Fionn lowered her head and sobbed. She was all alone. She was deeply upset to learn that her once loved and happy home was now destroyed and equally for pushing her best friends away.

"I'm sorry" she whispered, "I didn't mean for any of this to happen." She turned slowly and headed out to the forest to see the remains of her home. George and Arnie hadn't gone far, they were true friends and had hidden by a tree to watch over her.

"Fionn, we're your friends, why don't you let us help?" George said watching Fionn leave. Nothing more was said for a moment until Arnie started to whimper and moan feeling uncomfortable and awkward.

"Okay, we'll keep following her but let's keep out of sight until she really needs us. Okay Arnie?" Arnie barked in acknowledgement and licked George's face in agreement.

Chapter 11
The Witchfinder

Fionn wandered morosely through the rubble of the old shack, which she had called home for many years. Deep in thought and reflection, she hadn't heard the commotion stirring again down in the village below. She stopped for a moment to stare at her feline reflection in a puddle. "Hi there me…This could be the last time we see each other, so what do we do now? We've had a good few centuries and done almost anything that can be done as a cat…How easy would it be just to find a nice spot and stay there until we just disappear? Having never existed properly, nobody would really miss us, or… do we carry on now that we are so close? Shall we save the day and break the spell? Nothing to say for yourself eh?"

The puddle rippled as a soft breeze blew across its surface and a hazy figure of a man appeared behind her reflection.

"Fight on Fionn, be brave and free yourself. No matter what, I love you…my daughter."

"Father!"

For a second Fionn's heart lifted only to be lost again as she searched in the puddle, desperate for another glimpse. Moving closer, she hit out with a paw at the water trying to bring back the vision so that she might look upon her father's face once more. But there was nothing, the ripples faded and became still, as she sat in the wet grass with tears welling up in her eyes. Upon the ground next to her she noticed a faint light, she thought it odd as the sun had now set and there were no other light sources on the hillside to cause it. She wiped her eyes with a paw catching a glimpse of her shadow upon the floor and that of a man's next to her. She turned quickly expecting to see him standing there but there was no-one to be seen except for a brief glimmer of light disappearing into the forest fog, much like the glowing orb she had seen before, back at the library window.

Fionn picked herself up and began walking into the rolling fog that seeped between the forest trees with her head held high. She walked down the hillside encouraged by her father's words still echoing in her head and heart.

The village streets were deserted and eerily silent. Neither creature nor mouse could be seen or heard and the few scared villagers that remained cowered indoors with locked windows and bolted doors. The black night's rain had stopped and the moon was full, the quietness was unnerving. An unexpected voice gave her a surprise and she turned around.

"Good day to you witch. Did I come at a bad time?" It was The Witchfinder. "I now see that your mother was more devious than I had previously anticipated. Who would have guessed that such a vile, godless creature could spawn a child?" He hissed through his exposed teeth, his physical appearance letting moonlight pass through the holes in his body as he stood in the dark.

"Show yourself murderer! I will more than gladly place another scar on your face!"

"Angry words from such an insignificant creature, hardly deserving of the beating your mother was given before she admitted her guilt."

He walked into view.

"Why you..."

"Looks like Jack was right. You did come looking for this didn't you?" he held out his spindly wrist that had Fionn's necklace wrapped around it.

"What's the matter, witch? Still can't seem to find everything you are looking for? Here, let me help you!"

From every direction came a thick fog that rolled down the street towards Fionn, cutting off every exit and obscuring everything from view. The obscured shadow of the General was lit in part by the glowing streetlights. Each time Fionn tried to turn and face her assailant his shadow vanished. The fog began to shift and Fionn was confronted by a distorted view of the village, lit by a strange orange-yellow hue from lit torches. As the fog finally faded, she saw she was standing at the end of a large cobbled road, surrounded by a circle of shadows. The sky was filled with loud shouts and screams coming out of the dense vapour.

"Burn her!"

"Kill the witch!"

Fionn began to see people standing around the edges of the circle, holding pitchforks and waving them violently in the air.

Ahead, but still inside the wall of fog, she heard the crackle of flames and felt the intense heat coming from a huge fire. From the other side of the flames came The Witchfinder's voice.

"Move a little closer, witch. Come and meet the family!"

Fionn walked around the fire to see a woman's body appearing amongst the shimmering heat. Upon the bonfire, the woman struggled to get free of the ropes. The flames licked and tormented her body as the wooden stake burnt intensely. Her screams grew louder by the second. They were the screams of her mother.

"Halt!" yelled The Witchfinder.

Both the shouting and fire stopped instantly, as if frozen in time as the General moved closer to Fionn.

"Does this scene look familiar to you? I too remember it, witch. As your mother burned, I saw a cat watching. How fitting is it that it turned out to be you…the same black cat that scratched my face…" as he said this, he saw the hatred brewing in Fionn. "Ah! I see you remember. Good! Now perhaps, we should continue with your mother's trial?"

"Trial you say? I call it murder! And not just the murder of my mother and father, but the murder of all those that stood before you!" she extended her claws.

"First you're going to pay with blood and then I'm going to break this spell and hunt down every single one of your accomplices!"

The Witchfinder began to laugh and pace around Fionn.

"And how do you plan to do that? You'll never find Jack in time. And, you will never break the spell that binds you as that flea bitten animal. You will lose and disappear forever more, knowing that your one and only chance to break the spell and gain your retribution has gone. Nothing can save you now witch."

"Begin!" shouted The Witchfinder.

The fire continued to rage and erupt into higher flames, her mother's screams drowned out the crowd's shouting.

"This will be your trail by fire little witch!" he grabbed a nearby pitchfork and set alight the end.

Fionn ran for cover as The Witchfinder took aim. A second later he threw his first shot, which sparked on the cobbled ground and missed her by an inch. Without wasting any time the General let fly another shot, this flew past Fionn in a fiery blaze and stood upright in the ground in-between the cobbles in front of her.

"That was a little too close for comfort" she thought, darting away from a third attempt.

The little cat panted for breath but she kept showing her face to the Witchfinder, resolute and with no fear. The General picked up another pitchfork and ran towards her.

"Stand still witch! I'll make it quick!" The snarl of hate in his voice was quite evident.

Instead of running away, Fionn ran straight for him. He swiped at her with his pitchfork but hit the cobbles as sparks flew into the air. Blow after blow, came for Fionn, but she twisted and turned to dodge the flurry of attacks. She managed to jump onto the Witchfinder's bent knee and pounced upwards, over his shoulder, scratching wildly at his face as she had done before.

She landed shakily, noticing the cobbles were loose from the number of blows they had taken.

An idea came to her and, deciding to take a risk, she ran around the bonfire, close to it's flames. The Witchfinder gave chase as she'd hoped. She stopped, luring him in. He ran around the blaze halting directly in front of her. The fresh scratches on his face oozed and his eye gave a twitch of pain.

"What's the matter? No more sticks to throw?" taunted Fionn.

"You'll be sorry!" He warned with a pointed, rotting finger. "I won't be beaten by a cat!"

"Don't point that at me! I don't know where it's been." Jibed Fionn. "Do you like your new scratches? Come closer and I'll give you a few more!"

He lumbered towards Fionn in a fit of blind rage, gaining momentum with each stride he took. Charging wildly, he reached forward and hurled himself at her with outstretched arms, making a grab for her. She leapt out of the way at the very last moment. The Witchfinder treading upon the unsure cobbles stumbled, losing his balance and fell headfirst into the blazing bonfire.

"AHHHHHHHHHHHHHHHHHHHH!" he screamed in agony as the flames burnt into the remaining rotten meat upon his bones. Hand over hand he crawled out of the fire, still ablaze as pieces of his burnt skin dropped to the floor. His bony fingers gripped the cobbles drawing himself toward Fionn.

"Come here witch, feel what your mother felt within my fiery embrace and let us both journey to the afterlife together in blissful torment."

Fionn steadily drew away from his grasp as the fire destroyed the last of the muscle and tendons leaving all but the skeleton of the defeated Witchfinder. The skeleton hand gave one last reach out toward Fionn before it stopped dead and began to turn to ash. The skeletal frame crumbled, blowing away on the wind until there was barely anything left other than a pile of burnt remains as the ground began to tremble. The power that had once brought him to life, escaped in an explosion of light and flame.

The bonfire and people were gone and the fog immediately cleared. The air, no longer pungent and raw with the smell of burnt flesh, was now fresh and clean as the first drops of rain began to fall.

Fionn noticed her necklace on the floor undamaged. It must have fallen from his grip during the fight. She picked it up with her claws and pushed it over her head and wished. In the twinkling of an eye, she was human…

Chapter 12
The pumpkins

As the light dimmed, Fionn found herself sitting upright in the middle of the road, drenched by a raging thunderstorm that was now cascading on the village.

"Great, one extreme to the other!" She said rolling her eyes.

She could hear the distant chime of the church clock which now rang out 10 o'clock.

"I've got to get those pumpkins in place before it's too late." She ran to the Watermill. The river had swollen with the sudden heavy rainfall, ripping the mill's waterwheel off and sending it downstream. At the edge of the rising riverbank, Fionn could see the orange shapes of the pumpkins through the rain, it was clear they were close to being swept away. She ran and pulled each pumpkin away from the threat of the water and placed them inside the mill. As the lightning and thunder raged overhead, Fionn took a deep breath and set off across the village. She did this for each one and positioned them accordingly. Each pumpkin had to be placed in an exact spot, which followed the lay lines that ran through the village area. She dangled her necklace like a dowsing crystal, walking around each lay line source until the necklace glowed at it's strongest. She then began to position the pumpkins. One was placed by the town hall in the northwest, one by the witching stones in the northeast, another by the mansion gates to the north and one to the southwest in the churchyard. The fifth was placed by the remains of the witches shack in the south east, with the sixth at the heart of the village. This precise setting out had created the shape of a pentagram, that Fionn was now standing at the centre of. The pumpkins, powering up with energy, glowed orange, brightening to expose a Jack O' Lantern face.

Each quite different from the next, ignited with a magical flame that engulfed the entire lantern but did not burn it. Looking toward the church Fionn checked the time as the clock's bell rang out, 11pm.

Chapter 13
Final meeting

Fionn began to set off the final part of the trap in her plan to capture Jack. Each pumpkin was in its right place and, for her position at the heart of the pentagram, she began the incantation which she had memorised from her mother's spell book. Her necklace burnt with energy, showing it's light through her hands as the sixth pumpkin resonated in a strong orange hue. She repeated her chant over and over with more conviction in every breath; hands shaking and eyes turning white with the amount of immense power building up within. With one last effort of concentration the pumpkin erupted, shooting an orange beam of light into the night sky. One by one the others around the village followed suit like searchlights into space. Then the angle of the outer five beams lowered to connect to the pumpkin opposite, turning the whole village area into a huge pentagram. There was a mild quake beneath Fionn's feet as the outer beams began to shift again upward to join the central column of light.

When the six beams met the ground shook again as the energy of the Jack O' Lantern lights swelled into a large spherical bubble. The static energy disrupted all the electrical power within the village, cutting off all the house and street lights, leaving the sphere glowing in the night sky overhead as the only light source.

Fionn looked up at the orange ball, to see it was moving. From the top of the ball of energy rolled over a huge grinning face of a pumpkin lantern, which seemed to look over the entire village. Giving a big wide grin the huge face looked down upon Fionn, it's mouth opened as it fell to the ground illuminating the wet streets which reflected the orange light. Fionn covered herself as the huge lantern crashed harmlessly to the floor smashing into millions of smaller Jack O' Lantern bubbles, which seemed to hover in the air silently glowing. In the distance Jack stumbled through the streets as if in a drunken rage from the spell's power which surrounded him.

"What have you done?" he yelled at Fionn as he came into view. Fionn morphed back to her cat form and ran, heading for the mansion's old attic room. Jack chased after her, aiming volleys of powerful attack shots, which she tried to dodge by running through back streets and alleyways. Jack was throwing everything he could at her. Stray magic flew past hitting trees close to her, causing them to fall in her path. Cars exploded sending them into the air, as each bolt of energy struck, causing them to land on their roofs. Glass was shattering around Fionn, all the while Jack was gaining on her following closely even in his confused agitation, following her across the village toward the mansion.

Running swiftly through the main gates, Fionn gave a quick glance behind to check that Jack was still in pursuit. Storming through the front door she made a dash for the attic and hid. Jack too, still in a delirious rage, burst in through the mansion's doors and up the creaking staircase to the attic, searching for his prey. Fionn quickly shut the door behind him and sealed it with magic, trapping him within the portal's reach. Realisation brought him to his senses as Jack saw the spinning gateway in front of him. Accepting there is no way out he turned his furious gaze toward Fionn who was still by the door.

"YOU'LL PAY FOR THIS WITCH" he yelled and began to charge at her firing several more shots her way.

She dived for cover as she changed to human form. Jack's heavy footsteps rattled the old decayed floorboards as he searched for. He fired several more blasts smashing into stacked storage boxes sending dust clouds into the thick musty air. Others impacted against the ceiling shattering tiles, sending sharp shards shooting into the wooden floor. Fionn fired back, catching him square in the chest sending him reeling across the attic floor into a stack of old papers. He picked himself up, raising himself on to his knee and cackled,

"If that's all you've got little witch, one of us is in big trouble. Tell you what, I'll give you a clue…IT'S NOT ME, HA HA ha ha ha!"

He reared up from the floor and fired again. Fionn jumped out of the way but this time wasn't so lucky. Her leg was cut in several places by the splinters from a wooden box Jack had blown up.

"Oooohh oooh ohhhh" he belly laughed. "I bet that hurt!" he continued to gloat as he walked to where she had stood. Fionn had moved away, silently in pain, hiding behind a stack of old ornaments. She peered cautiously through the gaps, always keeping her eyes on Jack.

Jack was no fool. Having spent several lifetimes in the darkness, he knew when something or someone was nearby. He turned sharply to look directly at her and grinned.

"You'll have to do better than that witch!" he scoffed.

He sent out another burst of energy using the lantern's power, smashing into the boxes of junk, sending Fionn to the floor with a bump. On her back, she could see the church clock through a hole in the wall, 11.42pm. The clock's hand clicked to the next minute as Jack made his way through the debris to where Fionn lay winded and motionless.

"Had enough yet? In the next few minutes it will be too late and that's if you last that long."

Jack held out his lantern to launch another attack but Fionn had been waiting for the right moment. Quickly changing into a cat, she leapt out of the way to avoid the blast. She jumped up onto Jack's shoulder, scratching his face.

He flinched and she fell to the floor, claws extended.

She jumped again, this time deeply digging her claws into his shoulders. He let out a cry of agony and the cuts started to bleed.

65

"You know there is something worse than a paper cut... the scratch of a cat!" As she mocked him she changed back to a human. Jack laughed off her remark, "stupid creature, the fact that I am bleeding is merely proof that I am becoming mortal again and that you are running out of time."

Outside, storm clouds were engulfing the village, thunder boomed as the first flash of lightning bathed the old attic room. Jack faced Fionn but she was already attacking. Cupping her hands she threw two large blasts but this time she was not aiming at Jack. The shots rocked the lantern he carried and the magic ember splintered and scattered over the floor. Jack retaliated with shots of his own, but they carried less force than before. His power was beginning to fade. Jack dropped to knees in disbelief, surrounded by the glowing ember fragments.
"What have you done?" he screamed and he shook the lantern, trying to rejuvenate the ember back to it's full power again.
Fionn circled around for a better vantage point to strike, but Jack was quicker than she thought. Turning to Fionn he hit the floor sending a shockwave across the old wooden boards, which splintered as they travelled toward her finally knocking Fionn off her feet. With a wave of his hand a pile of splintered wood and rusty nails raised up in front of him then he fired them off toward Fionn. She was still on her side when the barrage of wood and nails flew at her. Grabbing a nearby suitcase, she shielded herself from being torn apart by the debris, the largest pieces piercing through the case just short of her face. In the distraction Jack had his eye on the hole in the roof as a means of escape. Fionn raced to her feet "Oh no you don't" she spat as she lifted the broken wood and nails with her magic and fired it toward the hole. The wood stuck itself to the wall as the nails flew past Jack, one of them clipping his arm, as it secured the wood tight over the escape route. Jack turned and hissed marching toward Fionn, knocking over any item in his way to the side or toward Fionn.

She staggered backward dodging each object thrown at her.

"You little witch, you're going to pay and your time is getting short. I lived for over 140 years tricking the Devil until I could last no longer thanks to another meddling witch. I've spent what feels like an eternity in that black hole he put me in with those unimaginable things. There is no day or night, no way of gauging the passing of time because you hold the only light source and everything that lives in that hole was attracted to it like a moth to a flame. The one thing that protected me was also the thing that made me a target."

Fionn fell to the floor as she stumbled over the missiles Jack had thrown at her. He stood over her leaning down screaming "I've waited so long for this moment and no one, not even you, is going to take it away from me." Fionn looked for something to fight with but there was nothing of use. As Jack drew close to her she pulled back her foot and kicked him between the legs then changed into a cat and ran off as Jack fell to the floor in pain. She circled around to the other end of the attic when she caught sight of the church clock,11:56pm when another flash of lightening struck close by.

Making the most of her advantage, Fionn renewed her attack by firing once again at Jack's ember. Further fragments littered the floor, glowing bright red, yellow and orange, hardening like crystallised candle flames. He returned fire, surge after surge, but he was evidently growing tired and weak with each depletion of the ember's power. The church clock's hand swept to 11:58. Fionn was losing time, fast. She changed back to a cat, making it easier to dodge the bursts of magic emerging from the lantern and jumped on to some nearby boxes to gain higher ground. Before she could turn to look around, she was sent to the floor with a bolt of power that penetrated the box below her with force.

The grinning silhouette of Jack closed in, lit only by the blue portal

behind him, the remains of his pumpkins orange ember and the sporadic thunder and lightning from the raging storm, which was growing in intensity. Fionn feared the worst and prepared herself. Suddenly from nowhere, George jumped from a high beam onto Jack's back. His claws ripped through his shirt, causing him to yell out in pain.

"NOW!" cried George. But as he spoke, he was knocked down by a clubbing blow from Jack. George slid across the floor from the impact as Jack turned back to focus his attention on Fionn. He was met by her human form, her face filled with anger caused by watching her friend get hurt. Fionn reared back with both hands cupped together to create a ball of energy, fizzing in her grasp. At point blank range and with all her might she punched it towards Jack. He reeled across the attic once more this time straight into the mouth of the spinning portal. Holding onto the edge of the doorway with his spindly fingers, Jack reached out with a last surge of power from the diminished ember and drew Fionn toward him. Her feet scraped across the floor as she managed to stop just short of him. With his bony fingers outstretched, he took one last swipe at her and grabbed the necklace from around her neck, but in doing so he lost his grip. Fionn changed quickly back into the little black cat. As he clutched his souvenir, Jack was pulled back into the portal.

"NOOOOOOOOOOOOOOOOOOOOOOO!" he screamed, as the portal spun faster, shrinking until it twirled into nothingness.

A sudden silence fell all around, even the storm outside came to an abrupt halt, the clouds began to disappear revealing clear full Halloween moonlight. It shone through the gaps in the attic roof and all the new holes obtained from the fight. From the corner of the room George appeared with a limp and Fionn rushed over to help give him support. "Oh George, thank you! I never would have been able to do this without you!" she gushed with sincerity.

"That's alright, what are friends for?" he replied with a wince of pain "I saw you lead Jack into the attic when I came to find you. It took me a while to find a way in. But what about your necklace? You won't be able to change back to a human without it!"

"Unless somehow I can break the spell…." she pondered.

In the distance the church clock tolled midnight.

"At least I'm still here…" she mustered.

There was a long pause before either spoke.

"George, listen, before…back at the hut…I'm sorry."

George smiled, "Don't worry, we're your friends, we'll always be there for each other."

Fionn grinned and purred with joy, rubbing her head against George's chin.

"So what now? Arnie's guarding the scout house and…" George was interrupted with a loud creak and rumble.

"Did you hear something or am I just hungry?" he asked.

The whole house moaned and shifted.

"I think we had better get out of here," said Fionn.

The house had been weakened by the force of the battle and the building was beginning to shake and rattle. A floorboard broke with a large snap, the doorways twisted and windows buckled shattering glass all around them. The two cats ran for their lives as the building started to collapse. They dived through a broken window, tumbling onto the grass, just in time to see the mansion crumble to dust and rubble behind them. There was nothing left standing. The two coughed, catching their breath as the ground below them continued shaking.

"Oh what now?" said Fionn.

The violent movement of the earth beneath them knocked George further down the sloping garden, as the ground around Fionn began to crack and tear itself apart. Shards of brilliant light shone out from the earth, trapping Fionn in a cage of light. George could hear Fionn crying out in pain.

Suddenly a booming voice came from all around them.

"The debt is paid," It echoed.

As the light faded, it left behind the human form of Fionn, lying motionless on the ground.

George approached her, nudging her with his nose. Fionn's eyes opened to see the face of her friend.

"You did it Fionn! You broke the spell!" shouted George with excitement.

Fionn lifted herself up from the wet grass and stood filled with joy. She looked down at her human hands and feet, grinning from ear to ear.

"Hey I've just had a great idea!" she said. Effortlessly, she turned back into a black cat at will.

George looked on puzzled. He wondered why Fionn had turned herself back into a cat…and then he grinned.

"Are you about to do what I think you're going to do?" he asked.

"Oh yes! Let's go have some fun!" she said in a mischievous tone.

Chapter 14
Goodbyes

Back in the alleyway, the local cats had gathered to discuss all of the strange occurrences. A tabby was telling the group about her adventure, but was cut off mid-sentence by the fat cat.

"Well! Well! Look who the cat's dragged in!"

George and Fionn walked up to the front of the group.

"So have you come to tell us that story again?" taunted the fat cat.

Before George turned to reply, he sneaked a grin toward Fionn.

"Well, my chubby feline friend, not only can we tell that story again but we have some pretty conclusive proof that will amaze your little green eyes."

The fat cat shuffled his weight around; reflecting on what George had just said and knowing all eyes were on him waiting for his response.

"Well then!" he said loudly to mask his awkwardness, "Let's see this proof of yours!"

All the other cats joined in with the nervous laughter as Fionn moved into the centre, ready to do her thing.

"I hope that after tonight, you will have seen enough to believe what I have always said."

The alleyway fell silent as all eyes were on Fionn.

"This is going to be good!" George said watching from a corner.

"Well? We don't have all night you know!" said the fat cat.

Fionn looked him dead in the eye, "Alright then!"

She closed her eyes and cast her spell, sending a swirl of light reaching higher and higher around her. The alleyway was aglow and the cats started to back off. There was no laughter in their panicked voices now. The fat cat began to tremble as the lights were stopping and a tall, dark human figure stood where a cat had once been. The group of cats stared with disbelief, the brave ones getting closer for a better look.

"Boo!" she menaced, leaning in towards the fat cat.

He screeched and hissed and arched his back, the remaining half of his tail filling out, hair on end. He ran towards the nearest fence, which took several attempts to get his fat belly over, his claws scraping frantically against the wood. The other cats also turned and fled, streaming out of the alleyway as fast as their little legs could carry them. Meanwhile, George rolled around on the floor in fits of laughter at their reaction. Fionn giggled too, after all those years of being picked on by her feline peers, she had finally got the better of them and it felt very good indeed. George picked himself up and walked over to Fionn grinning.

"George I…" said Fionn, but the words failed to come out as the laughter slowly stopped.

"You're going to say that you have to leave now, aren't you?"

Fionn nodded. "There's something I have to do and I think it's best if I go alone." She quivered as emotion built up inside her. "But I promise I will return one day…"

She lifted him off the ground and hugged him. Fionn carried him away from the alley, bathed in the glow of warm friendship.

"I need you both to guard that book until I come back, its important but I can't take it with me, can you and Arnie stay and do that for me?" she said tickling his ears and chin. George gave a silent nod and Fionn placed him back on the ground.

Slowly, Fionn walked down the street and left her friend behind. She kept her back turned to hide the tears running down her face. As he looked on, George failed to notice that Arnie had come to rest by his side.

"Bark!" said Arnie.

"Yeah, I know. I'm gonna miss her too."

The two friends sat and watched Fionn disappear into the night.

74

"She'll be back," George said, "She made a promise," he smiled up at Arnie and in his heart he knew that everything would turn out fine. The two turned to walk away, back to the book to keep it safe within the village just as George had promised. As they walked away, the duo faded away like ghosts into the night.

Epilogue
A new journey begins

As she stopped at the corner of the road, Fionn turned to give one last look at the place that had been her home for so many years. The houses were empty, the streets bare. Most people had fled to safety from the night's encounters while others were in hiding, not daring to show their faces at the window. She had been born here centuries ago and now finally she had broken the spell. It would take time for the village to heal itself. Fionn knew it would also be a while before she would return back here again as a new future now lay before her.

With a shiver, still not being used to her human lack of fur, Fionn waved her hands and a hip length black Jacket formed over her. Pulling the buttoned sides in close around her to keep warm she grinned and walked off into the darkness past the ruined mansion's grounds. Its remains covered with shards of Jacks ember, all glowing bright in the crisp night air as the large metal entrance gates now swung with ease in the cold gentle breeze. Looking into the distance, a faint glow beckoned to her from the witching stones on the hill.

"I'm coming mother, time to find out what comes next" she said aloud with a buzz of excitement and a new found optimism in her voice.

A light breeze blew as she walked uphill and, with her head full of thoughts, she walked quickly past a pumpkin lantern that had been abandoned on the pavement. The light within the pumpkin glowed dimly now, silently grinning as she passed by. The candlelight within flickered and died, the faint sound of Jack's laughter could be heard as the smoke wisped away into the cool night air.

But what is the end of one tale was to be the beginning of another....

Continued in Book2

Tail of a Witch
The Devils Game

Tail of a Witch
The Devils Game

by P.Simpson

Prologue

"Officer Hobs is that you?" shouted the reporter as he searched his pockets for anything to take a note with on the scraps of paper in his hand.

Hobs turned and rolled his eyes "Its two in the morning, I'm freezing out here all by myself and apart from what you can see without a flashlight and the fact I'm standing where a really large house use to be standing, how can I possibly help you Mckenzie, need a flashlight" he answered in a slightly sarcastic tone as he began to walk over to where Mckenzie stood. Hobs waited as the reporter finally produced a pen from his jacket pocket,

"Very funny Hobs, ha ha bet you're the life of the party. I only asked as I didn't see your car around but I heard your call out on the radio" joked Mckenzie back at him as he spoke out aloud as he began to write. "So, it's November 1st, A.M., there are people still out at parties or at least staggering back home from them which is where I should be SO, what can you tell me about what happened here", he finally asked, his pen hovering anxiously over the notepad.

Hobs sighed "For your record, we have ourselves a little mystery to solve and it would be better if you didn't write anything until we know what were dealing with, plus the fact what's it to do with you, don't you report for the paper in the next town."

The reporter was amused by the latter fact "the same as it's to do with you officer who also comes from the same town. Don't you find it strange that there's no one here, in the entire village?"

1

The officer turned to look back over his shoulder, the village was empty with doors open, windows broken and some but very few lights still left on, as if everyone had either run away at the same time or simply disappeared in a single night.

Turning to look the other way Hobs looked over the remains of what should be a mansion. Apart from the full moon light creeping from behind a cloud the whole floor area was aglow with orange embers scattered about the ground like glitter.

Hobs turned his gaze back to the reporter "I don't know what happened here but apart from being sent to find out what occurred you're the first person I've seen".

Mckenzie stepped forward to look at the glowing embers scattered around the ground.

"What are these" he asked Hobs.

"I don't know he replied" in a slightly hesitant manner "but I wouldn't touch it if I were you" he warned. Mckenzie seemed oblivious to the last comment as he crept ever closer to one of the glowing pieces and reached out to pick one up.

The ember felt warm in his hand and gave off a bright orange glow. The reporter inspected the piece closer, holding it between his fingers "You know it looks like burning wood but it feels smooth like a pebble, as if it was petrified, weird just, weird." As he looked at it further he noticed the glow spread into the tips of his fingers, he seemed transfixed as his skin burned but without pain going from red to black and charred, but still he looked on. The burning had taken his hand over, the ember still glowing in his finger tips as his skin cracked and the glow seemed to spread through the charred channels like the way molten lava would creep across the ground. The burning moved onward under Mckenzies clothes to appear again from his shirt collar and moving through his body, slowly roasting him alive but without the pain of heat, still transfixed unable to break his grasp in the ember. He looked over at the officer as if

2

in disbelief as the final wave of burning started to work its way up his neck and over his head. In the last few moments he turns his gaze back to the ember, not realizing it has fallen to the floor as his hand turned to ash. The look of panic fills his eyes as he looks upon officer Hobs who just stands there watching in the final moments as a gentle breeze blows and Mckenzie, silently screaming, slowly drifts away as paper ash would in the wind.

Hobs walks over to the spot where Mckenzie had been standing. Two burn marks glowed in the grass where his shoes had burned into the ground. Bending slightly Hobs reached out to pick up the same ember, and with a brief pause grabs it. Hobs looks back at the spot on the floor, flicking the ember into the air with his thumb like a penny, "I told you not to touch it, but people just don't listen." Picking up more of the larger pieces up he presses them hard in his hand to create one larger quartz shaped shard. Examining it closely he holds the ember shard, the glow lighting his face. Staring intensely, his gaze is interrupted by movement on the next hillside. He looks over peering through the moon lit night air at a formation of standing stones only to see the figure of a young woman staring back it him. Taking a few steps back, noticing that's she's being watched she turns with a flash of light, a cat is now in her place as it runs off in to the safety of nights cover.

Again Hobs smiles a wry grin. Suddenly from behind him comes a noise, this time the drum of helicopter blades beating the air. The clouds swirl in the downdraft as two more helicopters turn there spot lights upon the officer who quickly drops the large shard.

Several security types, all dressed in body armour with weapons surround him screaming at him, "Drop to your knees and hands in the air, NOW, NOW", Hobs stares back, unnerved by what is taking place as he slowly lowers to his knees and places his hands behind his head. Watching patiently he observes the third helicopter land as what seems to be a research team disembark. With white suits and full head gear they begin setting about with long claws on handles to collect the orange ember shards one at a time. The main research scientist makes his way over to the circle of security. Reaching down with his gloved hand he picks up the large ember by the side of the officer. Like a radio speaker the voice from the man inside the masked suit speaks "I'll get this bagged up with the rest of the science team, the rest of you secure the area and…" he pauses as if making a decision "Bag him and bring him with us." Hobs looks around as from behind him one of the security team takes the butt of the gun and knocks him out.

The sun breaks over the horizon in a golden blaze of light. Loading the unconscious officer aboard, the helicopters lift from the ground and scatter back into the safety of the night like cockroaches scurrying away from the dangers the light brings of being noticed. The grounds of the old mansion house are left clear of any ember that remains. The light of the new day highlights the devastation in the village. The sunlight reveals the one thing left behind from the scene that the darkness had covered up. A glare of light flares off the bare metal, a lone police car lies on it side, crumpled from its fall down the hillside behind the mansion grounds. From amongst the shadows, smashed glass and torn metal lies the bloodied hand of the officer formally know as Hobs.